W9-AQO-698

A NOTE TO PARENTS

Congratulations on choosing the best in educational materials for your child. By selecting top-quality McGraw-Hill products, you can be assured that the concepts used in our books will reinforce and enhance the skills that are being taught in classrooms nationwide.

And what better way to get young readers excited than with Mercer Mayer's Little Critter, a character loved by children everywhere? Our First Readers offer simple and engaging stories about Little Critter that children can read on their own. Each level incorporates reading skills, colorful illustrations, and challenging activities.

Level 1 – The stories are simple and use repetitive language. Illustrations are highly supportive.
Level 2 - The stories begin to grow in complexity. Language is still repetitive, but it is mixed with more challenging vocabulary.
Level 3 - The stories are more complex. Sentences are longer and more varied.

To help your child make the most of this book, look at the first few pictures in the story and discuss what is happening. Ask your child to predict where the story is going. Then, once your child has read the story, have him or her review the word list and do the activities. This will reinforce vocabulary words from the story and build reading comprehension.

You are your child's first and most influential teacher. No one knows your child the way you do. Tailor your time together to reinforce a newly acquired skill or to overcome a temporary stumbling block. Praise your child's progress and ideas, take delight in his or her imagination, and most of all, enjoy your time together!

Library of Congress Cataloging-in-Publication Data

Mayer, Mercer, 1934-
Tiger's birthday / by Mercer Mayer.
            p. cm. -- (First readers, skills and practice)
"Level 2, Grades PreK-1."
Summary: Little Critter goes to Tiger's birthday party and brings a kite as a present.
ISBN 1-57768-645-4 (HC), 1-57768-828-7 (PB)
[1. Birthdays—Fiction. 2. Parties—Fiction. 3. Kites—Fiction. 4. Tigers—Fiction.] I. Title. II.
Series.
PZ7.M462 Ti 2003
[E]--dc21
        2002008746

 Children's Publishing

Text Copyright © 2003 McGraw-Hill Children's Publishing.
Art Copyright © 2003 Mercer Mayer.

All rights reserved. Except as permitted under the United States Copyright Act, no part of this
publication may be reproduced or distributed in any form or by any means, or stored in a
database retrieval system, without prior written permission from the publisher, unless
otherwise indicated.
LITTLE CRITTER, MERCER MAYER'S LITTLE CRITTER and MERCER MAYER'S LITTLE CRITTER
logo are registered trademarks of Orchard House Licensing Company. All rights reserved.

Send all inquiries to:
McGraw-Hill Children's Publishing
8787 Orion Place
Columbus, OH 43240-4027

Printed in the United States of America.

1-57768-645-4

 A Big Tuna Trading Company, LLC/J. R. Sansevere Book

1 2 3 4 5 6 7 8 9 10 PHXBK 08 07 06 05 04 03

FIRST READERS

Level **2**   Grades **K–1**

TIGER'S BIRTHDAY

by Mercer Mayer

Mc Graw Hill **Children's Publishing**

Columbus, Ohio

Today I went to Tiger's birthday party. I made his present all by myself.

HAPPY BIRTHDAY TIGER!

PARTY HERE

I missed the donkey
by just a little bit.

7

Then, we played horseshoes.
I threw my horseshoe really far!

We made party hats, too.
Mine was really cool
except it was sort of sticky.

10

After that, a clown came
and made balloon animals.
I helped him make
a really big elephant for Tiger.

We sang Happy Birthday to Tiger. I sang as loudly as I could.

Tiger's mom made a great, big birthday cake. It was so yummy, I had to have three pieces.

Finally, it was time to open the presents.
Tiger liked mine so much, he wanted
to play with it right away.

14

15

We all took turns flying the kite I made.
Then it was time to go home.

16

DEFIANCE PUBLIC LIBRARY

I said thank you to Tiger and his mom.
I'm glad Tiger is my friend.

17

Word List

Read each word in the lists below. Then, find it in the story. Now, make up a new sentence using the word. Say your sentence out loud.

<u>Words I Know</u>
birthday
party
kite
home
friend

<u>Challenge Words</u>
donkey
horseshoes
sticky
elephant
pieces

Make a New Word

Use a separate sheet of paper for these activities.

Change one letter of the word cake to make a new word that goes with the picture.

cake

Change one letter of the word hats to make a new word that goes with the picture.

hats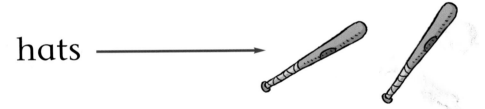

Change one letter of the word clown to make a new word that goes with the picture.

clown

Following Directions

Read the directions below. On a separate sheet of paper, draw the picture that is described.

1. Tiger had a three-layer birthday cake.

2. The bottom layer had yellow frosting with blue stripes.

3. The middle layer had green frosting with purple polka dots.

4. And the top layer had blue frosting with red stars.

Comprehension Quiz

Answer these questions. Try not to look back at the story.

Who was celebrating a birthday?

Name one of the games they played.

What balloon animal did the clown make for Tiger?

How many pieces of cake did Little Critter eat?

What gift did Little Critter make for Tiger?

Compound Words

Compound words are two words that make up one word.

Example:

snow + man = snowman

＋ = ?

＋ = ?

＋ = ?

Now find all 4 compound words in the story.

Rhyming Words

When Little Critter arrives at Tiger's party, Tiger is drinking from a can. On another sheet of paper, write down all the words you can think of that rhyme with can. Use the picture clues below to get started.

Answer Key

page 19
Make a New Word

cake ⟶ rake

hats ⟶ bats

clown ⟶ crown

page 20
Following Directions

page 21
Comprehension Quiz

Who was celebrating a birthday? Tiger

Name one of the games that they played. pin the tail on the donkey or horseshoes

What balloon animal did the clown make for Tiger? an elephant

How many pieces of cake did Little Critter eat? three

What gift did Little Critter make for Tiger? a kite

page 22
Compound Words

starfish
football
doorbell

Compound words from the story:
today
birthday
horseshoe
myself

page 23
Rhyming Words

man, pan, Dan, ban, fan, ran,
tan, van, clan, plan

24